UNDISCOVERED

A Collection of Short Stories

Timothy Trimble

"I just read 'UNDISCOVERED' by Timothy Trimble and I must admit - I truly like it! Reading this book was a unique feeling. I felt like the writer is my old friend and we are sitting in some cozy old house, drinking warm coffee and listening to some tales. The book is made of stories allowing me to travel from Leonardo da Vinci's time till today! Beautiful book indeed!" (Draga)

UNDISCOVERED

About the Author

TIMOTHY TRIMBLE is the author of Zegin's Adventures, the Air Born series, and many short stories. He's an author and technologist -basically a geek who likes to write. While he's been a non-fiction writer of computer related books and articles, his true love of writing is in science fiction and young adult urban fantasy. He lives in the Pacific Northwest, where the prevalence of coffee shops and hiking trails contribute to his inspiration.

You can visit him at the following locations:
- His website at www.timothytrimble.com
- His constant postings on Twitter at @timothytrimble,
- Good old Facebook.com/AuthorTimothyTrimble

UNDISCOVERED

Undiscovered

A Collection of Fanciful Stories by Timothy Trimble

Cover by Diren Yardimli, via BookCoverZone.com

First electronic edition – June 2017
First print edition - Feb. 2019

This is a collective work of fiction. All characters, events, names, products, and locations (real or not) in this story are not endorsements, are fictionalized, and any resemblance to reality is due to the author's vivid imagination.

UNDISCOVERED

Contents

UNDISCOVERED

Dedication

To Asia and Roman,

Thank you for your love and friendship.
You have enlightened my world.

UNDISCOVERED

Undiscovered

Why Undiscovered? Well, aside from the web-based audience who have seen some of these stories on Medium, Inkit, or OMNI, there has not been a way to see the full compilation of the stories I have exposed to the world. As a whole, they are undiscovered.

These stories also uncover a part of me as a writer. For the Zegin's Adventures stories and the Air Born series, I fully map out the story, its background, characters, and universe before I actually sit down and do the real writing. With the short stories, I take a totally different approach.

I'm always getting flooded with ideas. Some good, some not so good, and some are crazy exciting. When I get an idea for a story, I usually know right away if it's a complex tale which needs to be fully mapped out, or if it's to be a fanciful quest of discovery without knowing where it will lead me. These stories are those quests.

The spark of ideas sometimes come from observation. Examination of animal life and wondering what would happen if they were just a little smarter - Squirrels With

Guns. Some are ponderings about a historical genius with a twist of steampunk - The Wings of Leonardo. Others touch the concept of the difference between death or fading away - Invis. Sometimes I just need a way to vent my anger and frustrations with real life and the pain it brings to friends - Touched. And there is the fascination with time and portals to other universes - The Pendant and Jezi's Dilemma. My relationships with friends and associates who are autistic became the source for my desire to do research and mix in my interest in quantum entanglement - Meghan's Crayons.

Overall, Undiscovered provides me a vehicle for exposing me, my ideas, my inner being, and my quests as a writer. It is my hope these tales bring you as much joy in reading as they have brought me in writing them.

Enjoy the quests!

The Wings of Leonardo

Ever since I was a kid, I've had a fascination with Leonardo di Vinci. He was truly a genius and a "creative" who always sought to learn more. A common thread with many of my stories is the question, "What if?" What if Leonardo could see into the future? What if he could find out how his inventions were going to be put to use? What if I could write something with a bit of a steampunk feel?

***

Francesco stood on the very edge of the cliff, his arms spread wide, and his eyes open as wide as the distant sun above the horizon. The winds from the ocean washed over him with a constant intensity. He imagined his feet being lifted off the surface of the earth, becoming one with the wind, able to soar among the seagulls, which seemed to laugh at this wingless human - stuck to the ground. He

13

leaned slightly forward, letting the wind hold him back from the grip of gravity.

Leonardo grabbed Francesco by the back of his shirt, pulling him away from the precarious edge of the cliff. "Are you crazy?" Leonardo exclaimed. "If there was a pause in the wind you would surely be splattered on the rocks below, like the droppings from one of those birds."

"I could feel it, Leonardo," Francesco replied excitedly. "I know we were meant to fly. It's in my blood. I can feel it in the depths of my heart," he stated while pounding on his chest.

"Yes, yes," Leonardo responded, placing his hand on Francesco's shoulder. "I know how much you want to do this. But it's not ready! I still have much work to do, and with the tasks assigned to me by Cesare...," he shook his head. "I just don't know when I'll find the time." He hated to discourage Francesco but he knew he needed to check the future validity of his new invention before allowing it to be used.

Francesco shrugged his shoulders. "Yes, my head knows that you are right. My heart, however, wishes to fly," he sighed. "This is why you are good for me Leonardo. You keep me grounded when my head is in the clouds," he laughed.

Leonardo laughed along. "Come, come, my young seagull apprentice. We must return to Milan, for there is much work to be done." Quietly, he added out of earshot of Francesco, "Plus I need the forces of a good storm to allow me to see where this is going."

Leonardo double checked the terrain around him to make sure there were no curious onlookers to see him at his work. He hated to be out in the open like this, but he knew it was the only way to get his machine to show him what was to come. He knew a storm was brewing by the feel of the air and how his research papers felt. It was a mad rush to gather up his equipment, pack the horse, and ride out to the country. He knew his feeble excuse to Francesco would have to be explained at some point.

He did not fully understand why his vision machine worked the way it did. All he knew is with the right combination of magnetism, lenses, and the electric rays which were attracted to his iron stakes, connected by his thinly wound ropes - he would be able to peer into the future, to see what was yet to come. After many experiments, trials, and errors - he was able to figure out when in the future he could gaze, based on the number of iron stakes, their positions in the ground, and the ropes connecting them to his machine. He waited patiently as the winds increased and the dark clouds raced overhead.

The stakes were in the ground - distant enough to draw the rays away from him, yet close enough to push the energy into his machine. The pouring rain provided the link along the ropes to his device. The contraption of metal, magnets, and lenses, bound with leather and wood, was so heavy he had to devise a tripod to keep it steady. He took one more look at the sky and then he placed his face into the opening of the device. He pulled a black cape over the top of his head and the device, to prevent the light of the electric rays from blinding his view of the future. Then he waited.

As Leonardo waited, he pondered over the many times he was able to get a view of what was to come. The first time he was able to see the man made wall for storing up water. This aided him greatly when he was drawing the plans for providing water to the city of Florence all year long. *Cesare was very pleased*, he thought with a smile. However, the time he saw the man made bird was truly amazing. He would never forget the image of the winged structure as it flew across the sky. So straight and so rigid was its path, that Leonardo struggled for months to try and comprehend how such a device could stay aloft without the constant movement of the wings. He hoped that his own flying machine would be the beginning.

The sound of thunder roared from a electric ray strike just over the hills. Leonardo stared into the opening of the device, hoping a blink of his eyes would not cause him to miss a glimmer of the future. He could feel the energy in the air. The smell of ozone was crisp in his nostrils. His heart began to race with excitement and anticipation. He dared not to move or look outside of the cloak for fear of what he might miss. He was aiming for 400 to 500 years in the future this time. Farther than he had ventured to gaze before. To gaze any farther he would need more iron stakes and a second horse to carry them.

The crack of the electric ray was intense. Leonardo jumped slightly from the sudden noise. He could feel the hairs on his skin dance in the perspiration from the humidity. He could hear the sizzle of the electricity as it flittered through the air, providing the necessary energy for the magnetic fluctuations and distortions into the future. He stared intently into the lenses as the darkness turned into tunnels of light. The tunnels spun wildly and merged into a single point of light, which expanded to fill the lenses. Leonardo moaned with excitement as he watched the light turn into a distant view of clear sky. He could see tall structures extending high into the sky. Higher than any structure that he had seen before. He tried to peer into the sky above the buildings.

"Yes," Leonardo shouted as he caught a glimpse of what he was expecting. It would be the evolved result of his new invention. He watched as a single man made bird of straight wings fly over the top of the buildings. It passed by quickly. He was disappointed in the short duration of the view when suddenly he saw a flock of the large birds appear. They were flying in the shape of a large V. As hard as he tried, he was not able to count their numbers. One formation then two appeared. More came and passed over the buildings. Tiny seeds began to fall from the man made birds. Leonardo gasped at the number of seeds that appeared. Hundreds he guessed. The view of the sky was suddenly blocked by the appearance of stone and materials from the buildings. Smoke appeared and cleared, and appeared again. Leonardo struggled to see the cause of the distortion. Once again the smoke appeared and disappeared. He saw the buildings become torn and shattered. The image started to fade as the charge from the electric ray dissipated from his device.

A small electric ray reached out from the clouds above and struck the iron stakes. Leonardo praised God above for his extended time with the future. The image grew full in the lenses as Leonardo held his breath, for fear that his movement would take the future away. He watched as more seeds fell from the great birds in the sky. More smoke, flames, and shattered buildings appeared as Leonardo began to cry with the realization of what he was watching.

The man made birds were weapons! Weapons of mass destruction so great, it put the idea of his own wooden cannon house to shame. The birds dropped hundreds, or maybe thousands, of their cannon balls upon the city of the future. As the image started to fade, Leonardo caught one last look at something that shook his very being. A woman appeared in the center of the image. Her clothes tattered and ragged. Blood ran alongside the tears streaming from her eyes. In her arms was a young child, limp and lifeless. She seemed to be looking right at Leonardo through the image, pleading for his help, to make the pain go away.

The image slowly faded into blackness. He violently kicked at the tripod support for his machine, causing the bulk of the device to fall to the ground, the lenses shattering on impact. Leonardo stood and tore the black cape from the device and flung it behind him. He looked up into the pouring rain, hoping the intensity would wash away the image and the pain that it brought. He fell to his knees and cried as the vision of the child lingered in his mind.

Several days after Leonardo's use of the vision machine, Francesco bounded into the large workshop with the excited anticipation of a new adventure. "It's launch day, Leonardo," he stated as he looked around the workshop. He found Leonardo sitting at the great hearth, his back to Francesco. The flames of the hearth were larger than normal, creating an erie glow around Leonardo's silhouette. Leonardo didn't answer.

Francesco stepped over to the drawing table that Leonardo used for all of his designs. The drawings of the flying machine were no longer there. The inkwell was still moist with fresh ink and several quills sat on an old scratch parchment off to one side. Francesco could tell Leonardo had been drawing again. "You've been up all night?" he asked.

"Yes, my young apprentice," he replied without moving. "I'm afraid we are not going to fly today."

Francesco was dumbfounded. So much time and effort had gone into designing and building the flying machine. The winds were good and they had planned on testing it today. He ran across the room to the stables door and stopped at the opening. The flying machine was gone! His heart sank and tears welled up in his eyes. He knew Leonardo was prone to his own eccentricities but this was a major blow to scientific progress. He turned to face Leonardo. "But why, Leonardo?" he exclaimed. "I don't understand."

"The design was flawed," Leonardo answered. "It was not natural." He stood up with a rolled up parchment in one hand. He held it out for Francesco.

Francesco stepped over and took the roll from Leonardo. He rolled it out and held it in the air, letting the glow from the flames dance behind the drawing. The design was completely different from what he had seen before. Instead of the straight wings covered with stretched leather, these were more in the shape of an actual bird. Gone was the long round body for holding a man. All that was left was a harness with controls for moving the wings. "This does look more like a bird," Francesco stated. "You were so committed to the other design. We spent months working on it, building the frame, stretching the leather. Is it all gone?" Francesco asked, gazing at Leonardo.

"It made for a nice fire," Leonardo spread his hands at the hearth. His look was very distant, yet at peace.

"This is so different than the other. Are you sure that this will work? What was wrong with the other?" Francesco was intent on knowing why all his recent work had gone up in flames.

"It was not natural," Leonardo restated. "I feared that it would lead to a unnatural progression of events." He gazed at the fire in the hearth without really noticing the flames.

"Events?" Francesco asked. He was totally confused. He knew the capabilities of Leonardo were far beyond what he could do. Leonardo was the master builder, the architect, the Cardinal's personal designer.

21

Leonardo looked back at Francesco. "It was a design that was not meant to be!" he stated boldly. "If we are to create and design machines for mankind to use, then we have a responsibility. A responsibility to follow the natural progression as God intended. The other design would have lead to unnatural events which would have endangered our entire existence!" Leonardo gazed back at the fire. He looked as if he had aged another 10 years in just a few moments. The weight of the world was upon him.

Francesco was confused but also amazed. Here in front of him was the greatness of a man so intelligent, so creative, the likes of him the world had never seen before. Yet, he was just a man, burdened by the weight of his own creations. He pondered how just a man, could have such vision for the future? Francesco shook his head in amazement.

"This design," Francesco stated while holding the drawing back up in the air, "when do we begin?"

—

Meghan's Crayons

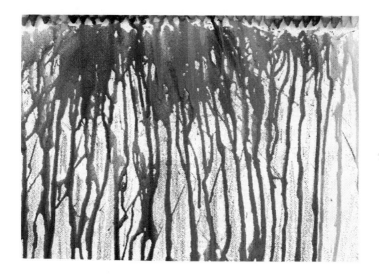

I've had the privilege, over the years, to have met some incredibly talented people who are autistic. Not only do they exhibit areas of incredible talent, but I always appreciate their sincerity, and their stance for what they believe in. I feel that my life has been enriched by these relationships and by being able to peek at what the human brain is capable of.

This story kept calling me. I knew I wanted to write it and I hesitated for quite awhile. I knew that as soon as I started it would nag me every possible moment until it was completed. I was right. There was a ton of research poured into this story and I lost a lot of sleep over it. The last paragraph was written when I arrived early for a lunch party with a dear visiting friend. "Where's Tim? Oh, he's in the living room, madly typing on his laptop."

I've dedicated this entire book to two dear friends who inspired me to write this story.

***

"Meghan is my middle name." The petite girl with the pixie black hair cut stated while staring up at the skylight window. She pointed at the sunbeam with her right index finger, tracing its edges down the wall and across the floor. Twirling strands of her hair with her left hand, she shifted in her wheelchair till her face glowed under the sunlight. Closing her eyes from the brightness, she smiled and started rocking side to side in her chair, as if a bubbly song played in her head.

"How long have you been here, Lindy?" Dr. Carpenter asked while flipping her computer tablet stylus through her fingers. She leaned back a little in her plush brown leather chair, making the leather squeak slightly. Looking over toward a one-way mirror in the wall, she raised her eyebrows, showing the camera and observers on the other side a confirmation of what she had told them all earlier. "I hope you're all patient cause this is going to take some time."

Lindy stopped rocking for a few seconds then continued while answering, "One twenty-nine by pie by pie."

Two men watched the young girl and her interviewer from the other side of the mirror. "What does that mean, Dr. Lee? By pie, by pie?" The clean cut man in a black suit asked. A red and white sticker badge above his left suit pocket showed a hand-written 'Dr. Jay Anderson' in thick black marker ink. He directed his question toward a bald man with a long and gray scraggly beard, wearing a white lab coat, standing next to him.

"It's how she answers anything numerical. It took us awhile to figure it out. We thought she was talking about food, but it's mathematical pi. Three point one four." He paused, watching Lindy and the doctor through the mirror, then continued. "It's 129 times pi, times pi. That comes to one thousand two hundred and seventy-five days. That's how long she has lived here with us."

"Three and a half years?" Jay asked.

"Yes," Dr. Lee responded. "She came here when she was eight. Her mother abandoned her when she was two. Social Services placed her in several foster homes over the years. When the last foster parents gave up, someone at Lindy's school decided to contact NAGC to have her tested."

"NAGC?"

"National Association for Gifted Children," Dr. Lee answered while running his fingers through the bottom of his beard.

"So, you called me because of my math and because she does calculations with pi?"

"Only partly, Dr. Anderson. Your math and your art. I saw your exhibit in Boston while you were at MIT."

"Wow. That was like twelve years ago," he replied with a smirk. "That was my last showing. My assignment at JPL doesn't give me any more time for it. But," he turned away from watching Lindy and gazed at Dr. Lee. "What does my art have to do with this?"

"Come. I'll show you."

—-

Dr. Jay Anderson was speechless. He stood in the middle of Lindy's bedroom. Hundreds of stubby crayons and discarded crayon paper littered the floor, bed tables, several chairs, and the entrance to her bathroom. The texture of the debris distracted him as he scooted several crayon stubs away from his feet, not wanting to crush any against the dark parquet wood.

"What the…" Jay stopped mid-sentence when he looked up from the floor to the walls of the room. From floor to ceiling, the walls were completely covered with highly detailed, but abstract drawings. "Wow," was all he could express as he gazed up at the ceiling, which was also thoroughly covered. He stood directly under the ceiling light fixture and gazed curiously at a small earth globe dangling under it. Slowly he spun around, noticing that the light switches and electrical outlets had also been utilized as her canvas.

Dr. Lee remained standing in the entrance, silently observing Jay's response to the incredible art of an eleven-year-old, highly autistic girl.

"Did she do all this?" Jay asked while slowly rotating, taking in the intricate details on every surface of the room.

"Yes. She started several years ago, after a field trip to Griffith Observatory." Dr. Lee walked to a wall and ran one hand gently across the texture of the drawings. "We called you because you're an artist, a mathematician, and an astrophysicist. We're assuming there's some kind of connection with astronomy, seeing how she insisted on hanging the globe knick-knack under the light fixture, and her choice of books," he added while pointing to Lindy's bedside table.

Jay walked over to the table and examined the cover of a book on top of a small stack. 'Fundamentals of Astrophysics, by Doctor Choudhuri' sat on top. The corners were worn from use. There were no crayon marks on the books. "She respects these books," he stated reflectively. "I have a copy of this one on the corner of my desk."

"Take a look at the next one." Dr. Lee added.

Jay moved the first book off the stack and instantly recognized the next cover. He let out a chuckle and stated, "My latest book. 'Quantum Entanglement's Applications for Communications'" He picked it up and placed the first book back on the stack. Opening the cover Jay stopped at the first page. "I signed this one?" He looked up at Dr. Lee with a puzzled look.

Dr. Lee nodded his head. "Lindy and I, with a few of my colleagues, attended your presentation at CIT. My assistant stood in line for over an hour to get that signature. Lindy reads through it at least once a month, though her first time through, it took several months and a lot of math. She wrote a bunch of the calculations out, studied them for hours, got a little excited, and wrote out more. Like she had discovered something."

"Excited?"

Dr. Lee chuckled. "Yeah. She claps. The more excited she gets, the longer she claps. It's a little over my head though. I'm not clear on what this whole quantum entanglement means."

"Ah," Jay responded, thumbing through the book. "Basically, via the use of entangled photons, or photons that have become related to each other, when we change the condition of the photons here, a related set of photons in England instantly change, and it happens faster than the speed of light." He glanced at the doctor to see if this was getting through to him. "I tell people it's like when you sneeze here in California and instantly your brother in England sneezes too." He paused again to let it all sink in. "It means we can communicate across long distances in an instant, regardless of the distance. But this," he stated while tapping on the book. "These are new formulas written by Lindy? That's interesting. I wrote a lot of theories and unsolved equations in this." He paused, removed his glasses, and placed one stem in his mouth. While gazing at the books on the table, he put his glasses back on. "Did anyone document the math she wrote in here?"

"We were preparing to and decided to just call you in. We didn't know she would cover it up?"

"What? Cover it up? The formulas in the book? They're not covered up. I'm confused. What is covered up?"

Dr. Lee pointed at one of the walls. "There's more math under the art."

Jay walked over to the wall and felt the texture of the thick crayon strokes. He scanned for any indication of writing under the drawings. Stepping back, he scanned the entire wall, and let out a sigh.

"I can't work with erased math." He shook his head and frowned. "Is there anything else?"

Dr. Lee stepped over to Jay, took the book from his hands, and turned the pages to the back. He pointed to the notes and calculations Lindy had written in the back of the book.

Jay grabbed the book back and studied the notes. "She noted grouping of photons for communications!" He paused and intently studied more notes and math. "We've just recently…" he stopped and ran a finger over one of Lindy's equations. He flipped through the note pages in the back of the book. "Wow," he stated and looked up at Dr. Lee.

"Keep going," Dr. Lee prompted. "The last page is the clincher," he added with a smirk.

Jay looked through more of the note pages. "More quantum equations," he mumbled and skipped to the very last page. "What is this?" He looked up at Dr. Lee and pointed at Lindy's writing on the last page and the inside cover.

"Check out the next book." Dr. Lee nodded his head toward the table.

Jay looked puzzled and turned toward the table. He paused and seemed stunned when he saw the next book. He slowly lifted it, careful to not disturb the hundreds of sticky notes and pieces of torn papers sticking out of its pages. "Burnham's Celestial Handbook."

Dr. Lee smiled and added, "She doesn't read it anymore, though she does like to tap on it now and then, while she's thinking, and staring up at her drawings." He looked up and waved his hand at the ceiling.

Jay gazed back up at the ceiling then asked, "Why doesn't she read it anymore?"

"She has it memorized," Dr. Lee stated in a slower pace and lower tone, knowing the impact it would have.

Jay widened his eyes, shook his head, and asked, "How soon can I start?"

"I'll introduce you this afternoon. I'm sure she'll remember you from the presentation. Though, she might not acknowledge it. She's pretty shy when it comes to new people and changes in her normal routines." The doctor let out a sigh and continued. "Time is of the essence, Dr. Anderson. She has the ability to contribute, to leave her mark upon us, upon the world, but it has to be now." He gazed at the walls, the ceiling, raised a hand as if to give focus to the entirety of the drawings, then added. "She only has about a year to live. It's Batten Disease."

—-

"Thank you for letting me visit you, Lindy," Jay stated. He shifted in his chair and rested one foot on top of a knee. Per instructions from Dr. Lee, he didn't stare directly at her, and he pretended to gaze around the room while he spoke. "You're a very good artist."

Lindy focused her full attention on a brand new box of crayons sitting on her bedside table. She wheeled over to the table, opened the lid of the box, and slowly tapped every single crayon with her finger as if to count it. Looking up from the box toward the ceiling, she tilted her head and slowly swayed side to side.

Jay watched her peripherally, watching for any indication of a connection with him. Dr. Lee had said it would take time. She would have to get used to having him around. He was hoping his name on one of her favorite books would spark something inside, and establish a common ground for discussion.

Lindy placed the box of crayons in her lap and wheeled to a corner of the room where a collapsible pole stood. She grabbed the pole and placed a crayon into the end. She tightened a turnable grip around the crayon, ripped some of the paper off the crayon, and discarded the paper, letting it fall to the floor.

Jay couldn't help but utter a silent "wow" to himself as he watched Lindy wheel to the middle of the room, extend the pole to full length, and use it to make elaborate crayon strokes onto the ceiling. Her strokes appeared to be random, yet her intensity showed they were planned, and with purpose. Each stroke blended with the art already there. Abstract, with a depth which gave the appearance of being able to reach into the thickness of the drawing. The colors blended gracefully with no sharp or discernible edges.

Hours passed by as if they were minutes as Jay found himself being pulled into the immensity of the ceiling art. Each stroke of color, each change to a new crayon, and the crushing of ignored scraps of crayon paper under the wheels of Lindy's electric chair, with the hum of the motors, and the slight clicking of the chair's joystick gripped by Lindy's left elbow. It all created a mesmerizing dance performed by Lindy as she painted with her crayons.

A tray of sandwiches and tea was brought in but sat untouched until the box of crayons was completely empty. The crayons had become a part of the mystical depth of the ceiling. Discarded crayon stubs and paper lay on the floor of the room like the remnants of a confetti parade.

Lindy sat quietly by her bedside table, reached for a sandwich, and slowly rocked side to side as she ate and gazed at the ceiling. After several bites, she rolled her head slightly with a slight side glance toward Jay. "Meghan is my middle name," she stated as if to introduce herself to the audience at the conclusion of her performance.

Jay smiled and nodded slightly at Lindy's of his existence. Instead of giving in to his desire to gaze at Lindy, now that they were on speaking terms, he forced his focus to the drawings on the ceiling. He couldn't make sense of the abstractness of it all, and yet, he marveled at the depth, thinking he could get pulled into the art itself.

Lindy finished her sandwich and sat quietly for the rest of the day, slowly rocking, and studying her work. Possibly plotting out her next box of crayons.

—-

The hours of Jay's observations turned into days, and the days turned into weeks. At the end of the month, after watching Lindy's daily routine, all he had gotten from her was a disclosure of her middle name during lunch, and watch her blow through a box of crayons every day. Each day he attempted to add a comment of praise for her art, an admiration for her technique, and sometimes a simple question. "What's your favorite color? Are you okay with me being here? Do you like music? Are there any stories you like to read?" He figured these questions might help her to come out of her shell a bit and maybe interact a little more, but after almost five weeks, nothing had changed.

Each afternoon, the facility staff would come and get Lindy, take her to therapy, medical checkups, and sometimes a recreational field trip to a park or another scientific discussion at one of the local universities. Jay would take advantage of this time to sit in her room, study the drawings, dictate his notes into his computer, try to make some sense of what Lindy was doing, and hoping for insight into the math she produced.

Today was no different, aside from the frustration he was feeling. He closed the lid of his laptop computer, took a deep breath, and chewed on a stem of his glasses while gazing about the room. "What am I missing?" He softly asked himself. "She knows the math," he mumbled. "The math," he repeated, stood, and retrieved his book from her table. He rapidly thumbed through it till he reached the theoretical equations reference. It was where he put the unsolved math, to be directed via footnotes from other sections of the book.

"Oh, my…" Jay slowly sat down on Lindy's bed and slid his finger along the pen scribblings on every white space of the pages. There were 17 pages in this section and each one had equations scribbled into the margins, the spaces around pictures, and even between some of the lines of printed formulas. Some of the printed formulas had been crossed out and inked arrows pointed to other equations in the margins. He slid his finger along one of the equations and traced an arrow to Lindy's math.

He quickly grabbed his cell phone and selected a number. He listened for a few seconds and waited for a beep. "Dr. Lee. We have a breakthrough. I need a large whiteboard on wheels and markers, as soon as possible." He hung up the call without a 'goodbye' and dove into a closer examination of the handwritten equations.

—-

Dr. Lee accompanied Lindy as she rolled into her room after her extended breakfast in the courtyard, which was intentionally delayed to give Jay time to prepare for her arrival.
She paused when she caught sight of the large whiteboard at the opposite end of her room.
Numerous equations filled the left half of the board. A

tray of markers and an eraser were below the board, which had been lowered enough to allow her to reach it from her wheelchair. Jay was in his usual chair, quietly observing, and not directly looking at her. A barely perceivable grin and a glint in his eyes made Dr. Lee chuckle.

"What?" Jay quietly responded.

Lindy slowly rolled toward the board, stopping several feet away from it, and gazed intently at the equations. She rolled her head and slightly rocked side to side, shifting her gaze between the board and her drawings on the walls. A short squeal of glee startled Jay and Dr. Lee. She applauded rapidly, no doubt excited with this new arrangement. Jay and Dr. Lee made eye contact and nodded in recognition of the major breakthrough.

 She stopped applauding, rolled forward, and grabbed a purple marker. Immediately she drew a line through a portion of an equation, drew an arrow below it, and started scribbling a new equation. Writing as fast as she could, she grunted, squealed, and mumbled to herself, possibly working out the equations.

Jay silently mouthed "What?" as he tried to grasp the new math he was seeing.

"Make sure you grab a picture of that when she's done," Dr. Lee stated as he turned and left.
Jay nodded, raised his smartphone, and started recording.

After several hours of equations and mumbling, Lindy stopped writing, placed a cap on the red marker she was currently holding and placed it in the tray below the board. She rolled back a few feet and slowly rocked side to side while pondering the full board of equations, arrows, circles, and strikeout lines.

Jay's phone battery had died long before she had finished. He remained in his chair, leaning forward, quietly mouthing the equations to himself, interspersed with long pauses as he worked out the math in his head. He looked puzzled at one of the equations. "Um…"

Lindy interrupted. "It's variable. Variable, not finite," she stated.

Jay shook his head. More from confusion rather than disagreeing. "How can that be variable?"

"It's variable, not finite," she stated. "Variable. Variable light controls variable spin. Spin. Spin is variable." She clapped her hands a couple times, no doubt happy about teaching the book writer something about his own math.

"Oh, my," Jay gasped and leaned back in his chair.

"Meghan good." She clapped a few more times. "Meghan's my middle name."

"Yes," Jay responded. "Meghan is good."

—-

Jay and Dr. Lee watched through the glass as two ICU nurses tended to Lindy. Multiple sensors attached to her head led to monitoring equipment next to her bed, a tube attached to her nose fed oxygen from an adapter in the wall, a nasogastric tube to her nose provided nourishment, and another dripped fluids via a catheter in her arm.

"This is significant, Dr. Lee." Jay ran one hand through his hair. "She was fine last night. She spoke to me. Explained her equation. She even clapped. I think she enjoyed showing me where my math was wrong."

"I know. It is frustrating, Doctor, but she's spent! Her seizure this morning was the most severe one yet.

We're not sure what the full impact will be until she wakes up."

They watched the nurses as they checked Lindy's monitors and made sure she was comfortable. One of them held her hand for a few minutes and silently mouthed "It's okay Lindy."

Jay crossed his arms, frowned, and shook his head.

—-

Days passed while Lindy slept in ICU. Jay hated the waiting, opting instead to pass the time sitting in her room, holding the book he had signed for her, and slowly thumbing through each page, examining the scribbled equations in the margins.

Based on what she had taught him, he wrote new math on the whiteboard, re-working his theories with her own equations. "Of course," he stated while stepping back away from the board. He snapped a picture of the board with his phone and sent it to his associates at JPL. He followed it up with a phone call.

He didn't even say hello. "Did you get it?" Waiting for the answer, he stepped up to the board and wrote some more equations. "Yes, that's correct. She says the rotation of the photons can be variable, depending on the intensity of the laser. We've only been looking for the occurrence and direction of the spin, not the rate of the spin, and when the rate of the spin has been changed, it changes which set of photons we are communicating with. We can change which photons in the universe we want to get messages from."

———

As more days passed while Lindy slept, Jay continued to pour over each scribble, note, and equation. A folding table became his desk in the middle of Lindy's bedroom. Her copy of his book laid open to the left of his laptop computer. Multiple printed out photos of Lindy's equations were taped to one side of the whiteboard and Jay's dry marker notes surrounded the pages, with lines and arrows pointing out how some photos were related to others, along with his notes on the right side of the whiteboard.

"I'm missing something," he stated to himself while thumbing back and forth between a couple pages in the back of Lindy's book. "These are quantum equations and different spin rates of grouped photons." Turning a page, he mumbled, "these are common celestial coordinates." His own sticky notes listed Ceres, M31, Alpha Centauri, Tau Ceti, and many others.

He grabbed his own personal copy of his book out of his wheeled travel bag, set it to the right of his laptop, and turned to the same pages in the back of the book. These had his own notes from different presentations and readings he had given over the past few years. He counted the note pages in the back of his book. There were no page numbers on these, designed to be blank note pages for anyone who bought his book. "I told the publisher I wanted 12 blank pages," he mumbled to himself.

He counted the pages in his book. "Twelve!' Grabbing Lindy's book, he placed it on top of his own and flipped through the pack pages. One through ten, he counted them. "Ten?" He counted again. "Ten." Once again, he slowly turned each page, this time sliding a fingertip along the edge of each page, feeling it's thickness. The next to the last page felt slightly thicker. He gave it a small twist between his thumb and index finger. The pages slid slightly but didn't separate. Gently inserting a fingernail into a tiny separation between the two pages, he slowly slid his finger along the edge of the pages. Finding the area of stickiness, Jay carefully pulled the two pages apart, slow enough to prevent tearing. "Wow," he stated while slowly spreading the pages. He sniffed a faded stain on the top left. "Strawberry jam," he chuckled while pulling out his smartphone. He snapped a couple pictures of the pages and then sent the best ones to his colleagues at JPL.

—

Dr. Lee and several nurses stood behind Jay as he sat next to Lindy. He gently lifted her left hand and he rubbed it between his. Her breathing was slow and shallow, with assistance from the medical ventilator. Jay grimaced each time the machine clicked followed by a rush of oxygen-rich air being pumped into her lungs.

Dr. Lee placed one hand on Jay's shoulder. "I'm sorry Dr. Anderson." He paused with a heavy sigh. "Her body is tired from the fight with the Batten disease. She suffered another seizure yesterday and we had to defib and then ventilate. It took over six minutes to get her back. But," he paused and choked back the next few words. "We've lost her. All, all brain function has ceased."

One of the nurses stifled back tears, covered her mouth, and left the room. Jay stood up, leaned over Lindy, and kissed her on the forehead. He whispered into her ear, "It's okay Lindy. I'll figure it out. Your math will change the universe." He stepped back and turned to Dr. Lee and the remaining nurse. "Meghan is her middle name," he stated and stepped out of the room.

—

Jay sat motionless in the middle of Lindy's bedroom with his body slumped low in his chair, and his head looking straight up. "Why the globe?" he mumbled to himself while staring at the small foam Earth globe she had picked up at the Observatory gift shop.

"Would you like to lie down Dr. Anderson?" Dr. Lee asked as he stepped into the room.
"Why the globe?" Jay asked.

Dr. Lee looked up at the globe and answered, "She loved astronomy. Anyone who can memorize a book of star charts has a serious addiction."

"Nope," Jay added. "I don't buy it. She was entirely focused on everything she did. She wouldn't want it for just a decoration. It serves a purpose." He sat up and spun his chair around slowly while studying the walls. "Do you have your penlight with you?"

Dr. Lee pulled it from the pocket of his lab coat and handed it to Jay.

"Excellent," Jay responded. "Can you turn the lights off please?"

Dr.. Lee stepped over to the switch and flipped it off.

Jay clicked on the penlight and spun his chair around slowly again, shining the light toward the walls. He stopped suddenly. "There!" he stated while standing up and walking to the wall. "A spot of wall." He kept the light on a very tiny spot on the wall where there were no crayon marks and the paint of the wall could be seen. "This is white paint," Jay added. "Do you have any ultraviolet light devices? For sanitizing?"

Dr. Lee didn't even answer as he quickly stepped out of the room. Jay searched the wall intently for any other spots showing through. He had found several more by the time Dr. Lee returned with a small ultraviolet bar lamp and an extension cord. Flipping on the room lights, Dr. Lee plugged in the cord, handed the lamp to Jay, showed him the switch, and walked over to close the room door and turn the lights off.

"Ready?" Dr. Lee asked.

Jay flipped on the lamp and nodded.

Dr. Lee turned off the lights and chuckled at the glow of Jay's white shirt.

"Come here doctor," Jay stated seriously. He placed a

hand over the lamp and waited for Dr. Lee. Once they stood together he added, "Now close your eyes for a few minutes and let them adjust to the darkness."

They both stood quietly while Jay whispered the seconds by tens as he counted them off in his head. "Ten, twenty, … one twenty, now."

"Wow," was all Dr. Lee could utter.

"All this time I had no idea what she was doing," Jay stated as they both slowly turned around in the center of the room and took in the immensity of what they were seeing.

Tens of thousands of tiny white dots and pinpoints within the walls could be seen from the glow of the ultraviolet light. A stellar map of stars, constellations, and the Milky Way galaxy enveloped them in the spatial darkness of Lindy's room.

"It's all accurate," Jay stated. "In relation to the globe of the Earth. She wasn't just drawing art. She was creating a map of our local universe. This is major. I'm going to need a few more months here Doctor."

"Of course," Dr. Lee responded. "I'll get the staff to remove furnishings. But, after I stay here a little while," he added, as a tear fell from one eye.

—

A red glow from an astronomy lamp illuminated the notes, books, and photos covering the folding table in the middle of Lindy's bedroom. All other furnishings had been removed, leaving all four walls fully exposed to the ultraviolet lamp mounted on an extended tripod next to the table. Hundreds of thin white threads extended from the small foam Earth globe to pins with note flags at different celestial bodies in the walls. Jay appreciated the view of the threads and the pins since they helped him perceive where the walls were. Prior to getting the pins mounted, he had fallen a couple times from being disoriented by the spatial depth of Lindy's star map.

An assistant, intentionally dressed in black, with thin white armbands, carefully worked along the walls, taking measurements between the map pins, and recited the numbers to Jay. He typed the measurements into his laptop and would then read back the figures and the calculated astronomical distances displayed on his red filtered laptop screen.

Someone knocked on the door and Jay responded with a "Come in, but be careful of the threads."

The door opened and a red glow from the replaced

hallway lights revealed the shadow of Dr. Lee as he entered the room. He stopped just inside the door and waited for it to close behind him. "How's the progress?" he asked while dodging some of the white threads, taking a seat next to Jay, and placing a two fresh cardboard cups of coffee on the table.

"We're just about done with documenting. This is the last set of threads for identifying the scale of Lindy's measurements." Jay answered with enthusiasm tinged with exhaustion.

"It has been a long fourteen months since Lindy left us." Dr. Lee stated. "Are you sure have everything she left for us?"

Jay grabbed one of the cups and took a sip before responding. "She hasn't left us, Doctor. We're going to be hearing from her for a very, long time. But, to answer your question, yes. I think this is it." He paused, looked up at the image of the Milky Way stretching across the ceiling. "Are you going to be comfortable with leaving this facility?"

"I will miss it," Dr. Lee answered. "I'll be sure to visit, once it has been opened to the public." He paused reflectively. "I accepted the President's appointment as Director of the Cure for Batten Foundation."

"I figured you would," Jay nodded appreciatively. "And I'm sure you'll figure it out. I'll be giving you plug at the President's press conference next week."

"No need to, Jay. Use the time to give all the credit to Lindy." He paused, took a deep breath, and sighed heavily. "Meghan's Crayons has changed the world."

———

The President of the United States approached the lectern. The sounds of camera shutters, rustling notepads, and reporters whispering to their live feeds permeated the room as he started to speak.

"Normally, I stand at this microphone, to address the people of the United States. Today, I stand here to address not only the world but the universe."

Gasps and murmurs in the room grew. The President raised his hands and signaled for quiet. "What I'm about to announce will change our world forever. In fact, it has already. And to signify the importance of this, many of the world's leaders are tied into this conference, including President Jinping of China, President Putin of Russia, UK Prime Minister May, and many others who I would like to name, but time is of the essence." He paused and waited for quiet.

"To my right, is a man you've never met before." He gestured to his right. "This is Doctor Jay Anderson, formerly with the Jet Propulsion Laboratories, who is now the newly appointed Director of Interstellar Communications." He waited for the questioning whispers and undertone conversations to die down. "Since much of what needs to be presented is over my head, I present to you, Dr. Anderson."

Jay walked over to the President, shook his hand, received a shoulder slap, and then stepped up to the microphone. "Two years ago, I had the pleasure of being introduced to a highly autistic, eleven-year-old girl, Lindy Meghan Lewis, who knew more about math, astrophysics, and quantum entanglement, than I could ever know. She liked to remind me on a regular basis that 'Meghan is her middle name.'

"Sadly, she has left us as a victim of Batten Disease. However, it doesn't mean she no longer speaks to us. Without getting too technical for the general public, she left behind a wealth of scientific discovery which far surpassed anything we have ever come across before. Her grasp of astrophysics and quantum entanglement has provided us with a method of communicating instantaneously with other intelligent life throughout the universe."

The roar of gasps, comments, discussions, and

camera shutters erupted to a noise piercing level. The President stepped to the mic and interrupted. "Please, please, everyone. Let's have some quiet and let Dr. Anderson finish his statement.

Jay held his composure and waited for the room to become quieter. "Thank you, Mr. President." He paused then continued. "The science of quantum entanglement provides us with the ability to instantly change how related photons act regardless of distance. For example: Imagine you sneeze and your cousin in London sneezes at the exact same time." A few reporters chuckled and stopped short from the overwhelming mood of seriousness.

Jay continued. "We know we can change the status of a group of photons in England by firing a laser at a group of photons in Seattle, regardless of the distance, and exceeding the speed of light. Because of Lindy's efforts, we learned how to listen for life in the universe by watching for changes in photons, and she taught us how to manipulate the photons to send our own communications out, and in which direction. Thanks to Lindy, we established the first contact with intelligent life last month."

Everyone in the room was stunned. Only the sound of camera shutters could be heard while they waited for him to continue.

"As far as we can tell from the immense stellar map Lindy left for us, we have determined our first contact was with the star system Vega. We detected a constant pattern of photon changes followed by a single set of numbers ranging from one to thirty-seven, followed by a fourteen-minute pause. It was obvious they were telling us how to use our own alphabet, the numbers zero through nine, and a blank space. It took us several days of analysis to actually determine the significance." He paused again to wait for the room to quiet down.

"We returned the same sequence to them during one of the fourteen-minute pauses. The next pattern response we received stated the following:" He paused and made sure he had everyone's attention. "We hear you. We are peace. We help. Next will be one your solar." The room erupted into noise again until the President signaled for everyone to get quiet.

Jay continued. "This means that one year from last month, they will communicate with us again. We have received no other communications since then. The photons are silent." He paused and took in the astonished looks, open mouths, and questioning expressions. "I will now entertain your questions."

Everyone in the room raised their hands at the same

time while shouting 'Doctor Anderson'.
Jay pointed at one of the reporters in the audience.
"The reporter in the blue dress."

The reporter stood then asked, "You said Lindy left you a stellar map. Can we see it?"

Jay responded, "I'm very happy you asked that. Lindy covered all of the walls and the ceiling of her bedroom with crayon art. It took me months to figure out what she was doing. That room will be part of the soon to be opened Center for the Study of Interstellar Communications. The exhibit will be called, "Meghan's Crayons." He paused and focused on the fond memories he had of spending time talking and examining her art. Before he called on the next reporter he added, "That is where she touched my very soul and if you see it in person, she will touch yours as well. Next question?"

—

Touched

Every now and then a story is written out of necessity. Such is the case with "Touched." Someone I know was in an abusive relationship. She never came right out and told me, but I could read the signs, and unfortunately, there was nothing I could do. In my frustration of wanting to help I wrote this story.

Of all of my short stories, this one has become the most popular with my readers. There is so much in this story that deviates from my normal story telling. It's the darkest story I've ever written and it's the first time I've written a story in first person point of view. I did a reading of this story with a group of close friends after a dinner party, shortly after writing it. It was the first time I ever had a completely silent room when I finished reading. When I do public book readings for one of my books and get into Q&A, I usually get asked when am I going to turn this one into a full length novel.

There is absolutely no reason to strike out in anger against a loved one. If only I had the touch.

***

I watched from the corner booth table as he hit her across the face. It made me cringe. It always does. I used to turn away and ignore it, but watching helped me to build up the anger, which also helps with my touch.

I could see the tears form in her eyes, the undeserved shame on her face. If she showed anger, there was a chance for the two of them. She would be angry enough to fight back, to fix the problem, or to leave. But, when the look was shame or guilt, it usually meant it was a long term problem. The man had literally beaten her down into submission—she was convinced she had done something wrong to provoke the abuse, that he was in charge, and her only role in life was to try and make him stay happy, to not be angry. Maybe it was leftover from her childhood. Possibly an abusive father, or even a mother, who made themselves feel somehow elevated in the world when they took to demeaning their children. I don't know. I wasn't there. All I know is from what I was currently seeing.

It's always hard for me to wait for the right moment. I needed to be sure this would be for the best. I knew it would be soon.

She started to get up, to head to the restroom. The man grabbed her arm and forced her back into the booth seat next to him. She cried some more, wiped her mascara with a napkin, smearing it down one cheek. She seemed to be good at this maneuver. He was too drunk to know any better. She pointed at her face and the man waved her off to the restroom to clean herself up. It was followed by finger-pointing, no doubt to remind her she had better be back soon.

I never wanted the abused to see me, to determine there was any connection between me and their situation. That would just lead to further complications and explanations they would never be able to understand anyway. Likewise with anyone else in the area. There were no cameras to take note. The rest of the patrons were too busy with their own drinks, conversations, and the blaring sports channels on the big screens. A waitress stopped by the man's table and he signaled for 2 more drinks. No words exchanged and the waitress walked off. No one else was looking. It was time.

I got up from my dark corner table, walked directly over to the man. We didn't speak and I didn't want to look angry or hostile. My only look as I touched his shoulder was one of intense concern. Not just concern for how the woman would carry on her life afterward, but concern for how the man would adjust to his new environment. Feeling my touch on his shoulder, he turned to look at me. Most likely expecting to see the waitress. His look turned to questioning and I reached up and touched him between the eyes and above his nose. He instantly felt the surge of energy and didn't have a chance to respond in any way. Within a few seconds, he had faded into nothingness. The shape of his butt slowly faded from the vinyl booth seat as I walked back to my corner table.

The waitress came back and placed two drinks on the table and left. A few minutes later the woman came back from the restroom. She looked puzzled and glanced toward the men's restroom door, thinking the man must have gone to relieve himself. I lingered for a few more minutes while I finished my glass of beer. Such an awful drink as it is. I have no understanding as to why these people even find enjoyment in this. Maybe they'll eventually learn to find pleasure in other things, once the population of the angry ones dwindled more.

I tossed a couple strips of printed paper down on the table and left through the front door, confident I selected the right time for this woman and her abusive mate. I reached for my modified cell phone and called my contact on Modrass. "Did you get the delivery?"

"Yes, he is here. He looks like he'll be a good fit for what we need. Thanks. I'll be sure to load your credits by moon fall."

I clicked off the phone as soon as I heard the commotion on the street corner. A man was grabbing someone by the hair and exclaiming human profanities. Sigh. It's going to be a busy night.

—

UNDISCOVERED

Squirrels With Guns

I threw this together during my lunch break one day. I have always been fascinated with animals and have wondered what they would be like if they were just a little bit smarter. This is a short read with a little light humor, but in concept could turn into a major disaster story. Enjoy.

***

The man reached into the trunk of his car, grabbing the last bag of groceries. He stepped back with the bag in one hand and started to close the trunk lid when he felt a nudge on the back of his leg, just below the knee. He turned, expecting to see a toy left by one of the neighbor kids.

What he did see caused the hairs on the back of his neck to stand up. His heart rate instantly doubled as a red laser beam slowly moved up his face and stopped in the center of his forehead.

The gray squirrel was standing on its hind legs. A flak jacket covered its chest but dropped down almost to its feet. Either it was a very poor fit or possibly a modified rain coat painted to match the local brush, and with the sleeves ripped out. But the most important accouterment was the miniature M16 with the laser targeting scope.

The silence seemed to last forever as the man contemplated his options. He knew how reactionary the squirrels could be. A slight twitch and he could be a bloody corpse laying in the driveway. Assassinated by a squirrel.

The man drew in a breath in preparation of asking the squirrel what he wanted. He assumed the squirrel was a "he". He wondered if the females were this aggressive?

Before he could utter a "What…" the squirrel spoke in a high-pitched gravelly voice, "Peanuts! Gimme peanuts!" The squirrel's tail started twitching up and down, smacking the driveway without a sound. The squirrel continued rapidly, "Peanuts, peanuts! I'll shoot. Gimme peanuts!"

The man slowly moved his free hand out toward the

squirrel — palm facing out. "D' don't don't shoot!" he responded in as mild a voice as he could muster.

He slowly kneeled down and placed the bag on the driveway. He reached into the bag and pulled out the full two pound, clear bag, of roasted and shelled peanuts.

The squirrel's tail twitched even more rapidly as he watched the man place the bag of peanuts onto the driveway.

The bushes off to the side of the driveway seemed to explode as four more squirrels ran out. They were chattering rapidly as they scrambled over to the bag of peanuts — each one grabbing a corner of the bag. The squirrel with the gun kept the laser dot pointed on the man's forehead as the four other squirrels ran off with the bag of peanuts.

The squirrel with the gun slowly backed away from the man — the gun still pointed at the man's forehead. When it was out of kicking distance the squirrel quickly turned and dove off into the bushes.

The man paused for a minute to make sure the last of the squirrels were gone. He picked up the bag of groceries and reached inside to pull out another two-pound bag of peanuts. As he turned and closed the trunk lid of the car, he chuckled to himself, "You'd think they would learn by now I always keep a spare." He laughed as he disappeared into the house.

—

Jezi's Dilemma

This story started as a submission to the Edmonds Write on the Sound Writers Conference. Each year a theme is presented and the story has to be 1500 words or less. The theme for this one was Seattle, which I managed to throw in. (Heh.) I think of this story as my mis-understood child. Out of all my short stories, this one gets the least amount of love from my readers. I'm not sure why. But I think it's special and it allows me to ask another "What if?" question. What if space commuter travel required sleeping in stasis? What if your stasis pod was mis-routed? One missed stasis port could ruin your whole decade.

***

"What do you mean I'm not on Alcore? I spent twelve hundred cred to get to Alcore and now you're telling me I'm on some planet called Tristola?" Jezi tried to be loud enough to make a small scene, but she didn't want to be so loud enough for the Port Authorities to come and investigate.

"I'm sorry," the flustered flight agent responded. "It seems you were transferred to an incorrect jumper at Blanifia while you were in stasis." The attendant tried to give her best apologetic smile through her heads up display. "We can offer you full compensation and a free ticket to any destination within twelve parsecs."

Jezi was in total disbelief. She felt like pulling all her hair out while screaming and running circles around the terminal lobby, but she knew it wouldn't solve anything. Not to mention someone would probably post it on the Uni-web. She took a deep breath before responding. "And how long ago did that happen?"

The attendant focused on her display while answering, "Um, it looks like 3 terra months ago. Would you like your compensation now?"

Jezi was in shock. "Three months ago? I should have

been on Alcore over two months ago!" She stood there for a long uncomfortable minute, staring at the attendant. She was hoping this was just a dream and she would wake up soon to find herself on Alcore.

"Would you like your compensation now?" the attendant asked again while glancing past Jezi at the other people standing in line.

Jezi turned around to look behind then back at the attendant. Without a word, she placed her hand on the raised palm display. After several seconds the display beeped and showed the transfer was complete. Jezi looked at the skin embedded display in her palm to confirm.
"Thank you for flying with SolSpace, and I hope you have a pleasant flight, wherever your destination may be." The attendant stated and looked at the next customer in line.

Jezi walked away from the ticket counter, still stunned at her predicament. Her hover pack followed closely behind. She tried to remember what it was it the attendant said - destination? There was no need to go to Alcore now. Her assignment to cover the birth of a new Standerbeast was way past being overdue. No need to contact her editor either. There wouldn't be any chance of getting another freelance assignment from him again. She continued slowly walking, in a daze, not really heading in any specific direction. She didn't know where she would go or where she could get another assignment. She needed a fresh start and maybe this was the opportunity.

"Yes, you could be enjoying the sun filled purple skies and beautiful golden waters of Tenaria." The display sign spoke to her as she came within its advertising perimeter. Jezi stopped to look at the holo display. Her hover pack bumped lightly into the back of her legs.

Sensing she was watching, the display continued, "Imagine yourself laying on the beaches of Tenaria, the radiant warmth of the dual suns giving you a glowing tan, followed by a multi-course dinner of our highly rated and unique seafoods, and finish with a perfect night of dancing in the infamous clubs of Landon Beach.

She paused and gave it a thought, then responded, "Nah!"

The display switched to a view of rugged mountains and sheer cliffs. "Wouldn't it be wonderful to find yourself among the breathtaking beauty of the peaks and..." Jezi pointed at the display and slid her pointed finger to the right. The display of the mountains slid off the side of the display and a new image slid in from the left. "Only a terra month of stasis sits between you and the casinos of..." She flicked her hand to the right and watched as the display updated.

The next image of the display seemed to reach out and surround Jezi. A deep blue sky with scattered puffs of white clouds hovered above with a rocky shore along a serene body of water seemed to be just below her feet. She could hear the lapping of the shallow waves of water kissing the sand and rocks. A strange gray and white creature flew overhead, calling out to her in a high-pitched squeal, almost as if it was singing to her. The display spoke. Not the rapid sales pitch of the previous offers. This time it was a kind and gentle voice, male, with a hint of an accent she had not heard before.

"Some call it Terra. Others refer to it as its ancient name of Earth. Regardless of what name you use, there is no denying this beautiful planet, now called Trinth, is the ultimate destination for those who are seeking peace, tranquility, and the experience of a lifetime."

Jezi didn't know if it was the voice or the sheer beauty of the projected holographic image that appealed to her. She knew she was going to go there. There was no forethought, hesitation, or a hint of trepidation. She had dreamed of this place.

The image seemed to lift her above the beach and the water. It moved, giving her the sense she was flying above the water. The sensation was so real she had to steady herself, to keep from falling forward, as she leaned in the direction of the movement. Lush green islands rose up in the distance. Towering peaks of mountains arose on the horizon, topped with a pristine white so bright, it seemed the sun had scattered its constant fusion of energy there.

The voice continued, "Once a place of savage wars and selfish plundering, the inhabitants of this beautiful world turned their attention to restoring Trinth back to the condition it was in before the plundering. It has become the example of how humankind could co-exist with their native environments while carrying forth their message of peace, prosperity, and expansion to the stars of the universe. Would you like to learn more about Trinth?"

All Jezi could do was slightly nod her head as she was whisked away into the beautiful skies of Trinth. After a long pause, she realized she needed to verbally respond. "Yes," she said.

"I am interested."

The display changed to show the man behind the

voice. His hair was long, silken, and black - a perfect match for the ebony black pupils of his eyes. His smile was sincere and it highlighted the lines of kindness around his eyes. Jezi figured him to be in his thirties, in terra years. He had an appealing face without being overly handsome and a ruggedness in his stance and composure. This was not some actor or model, Jezi thought to herself. This was a real Terranian.

The man pointed to a view of the Trinth travel counter and then pointed in the general direction within the terminal. He looked directly at Jezi and concluded, "Would you like to see this presentation again?"

She was tempted to say yes, just to experience it again. She turned and headed in the direction pointed out by the native Terranian, her hover pack following closely behind.

--

As Jezi stepped up to the counter a holo image of the flight agent appeared. "May I help you?" asked the attendant.

"I would like to go there, to Trinth," she replied while pointing to one of the travel holo displays behind the attendant.

"Excellent. I can help you with that. May I have your identification and travel permits please?"

Jezi pressed her palm up to the scanner on the counter. As the system read her information, she could see the attendant's smile turn into a look of concern. A subtle beep indicated the scanner was done. "Is there a problem?" Jezi asked the attendant.

"Well, it looks like you have a voucher for up to twelve parsecs. I'm afraid that is not enough for a ticket to Trinth," the attendant paused. "Unless you have the funds for extending the voucher? It would be twelve thousand creds to the additional thirty parsecs."

"Twelve thousand creds?" Jezi exclaimed. She only had a little over thirteen thousand in her account. It was her whole life savings. "Do I take the leap?" she asked herself, not really intending to ask the attendant.

The attendant looked at her display then back up at Jezi. "It's two years of stasis, some serious money, and I'm assuming this is a impulse decision," the attendant replied.

Jezi pondered what she was about to do. A fresh start. Years away from friends and family. Back to comfortable, familiar? Or off to seek adventure, and new stories to write? "What's the name of the city where I'll be landing?" she asked the attendant. Looking at her display, the attendant replied, "Seattle."

"That's a nice name." Jezi pondered this decision, closed her eyes, and placed her hand on the scanner. "One ticket to Trinth."

—

UNDISCOVERED

Invis

This is one of those short stories that just happened during a lunch break. It's another "What if?" story. What if there was a disease that caused someone to ~~become~~ become transparent as they got older, but it also extended their life? I enjoyed writing this one and I have received a lot of good feedback from other readers. Everyone seems to get something metaphorical out of it, even though that was not my intent. I would love to turn this into a full length novel or series.

***

The forest was especially active today. Wyce could feel the flow of the life forces through the trees, ferns, and animal life. If he closed his eyes and focused he could pinpoint insects within a short radius. He breathed deeply and took in the rich smell of the plants and moisture around him. It was his favorite sitting spot in the immense forest - his rump in the damp carpet of leaves and his back against a tree stump as old as he was. Quiet enough to allow him to focus on how good his life had been. Yes, this was exactly where he wanted to be at this stage of his long enduring life. At the ripe old age of 176, his life had been full even though it was limited by his disease. His mind was still sharp. He had plenty of time for reflection back to his younger days.

Wyce was only 6 when the doctors discovered he had contracted Invis. Even when he was young he was able to tell he was different. He knew from how he was treated by his parents, since that day at the clinic. He really didn't understand why until the symptoms started to become more pronounced when he was 10. Aside from the semi-transparency of his skin, he could sense the flow of electricity. It didn't hurt back then. In fact, he remembered he had a lot of fun with knowing how much force was flowing when the holovid was on, or when the replaprinter was generating dinner. But he was sent away before the real pain could begin.

It was pretty difficult being 13 and being told he had to move away for his own safety and comfort. His parents and the medbot tried to explain it would be for the best, to be away from the electricity. They focused on the good that would come from his disease. He could be in touch with nature. His life would be prolonged, being able to live over 150 years - unlike the 70 or 80 for the non-infected. He would have a life surrounded by others like himself. His parents explained what was happening to him, due to this incurable disease. He would eventually vanish. To where - they couldn't say. The only answer they could give was it would be peaceful and painless. They were not sure if it was death. Their positive spin was they felt he would continue on into a different dimension - kind of a parallel world with others like him. That was the last time he saw his parents.

They were right about his having a good life. The Territory was immense, beautiful, and nothing like the life he had back in New Chicago. He had a bit of withdrawal from leaving behind his cyber games, holovid, and everything requiring electricity. He couldn't even keep a comms tag - calls to the world outside the Territory were not possible. Sure, there were some who tried to smuggle stuff in. But the elders would sense the devices, confiscate, and destroy them, and there were the intense moments of depression when he thought about his parents, family members, and friends.

He eventually discovered that life without electricity was a true pleasure. What he once had only seen in the museums, he could now actually touch and own. Books, a bicycle, a chess set, pencils, pens, paper, and scissors. Ah, the marvel of scissors! Nothing like the automated laser cutters used outside the territory. As he grew older he discovered he was actually quite good at carving and sculpting. Intricate designs and portraits in wood would capture the attention of all who visited his studio. When he wasn't carving, or sitting in the forest, he could be found in the Great Library - reading everything he could get his hands on.

He fed his thirst for knowledge by learning as much as he could about Invis. Nothing he read could tell him how it was spread, or how it would pick its victims. He never really considered himself to be a victim, but rather, he felt it was a blessing. Invis never appeared until after the food wars of 2054. Some scientists speculated about it being a genetically evolved virus from food generation experimentation. Others thought it rode along with the return of the first Mars explorers. There were those who thought it was either a curse or a blessing from their spiritual entity. All he could learn about it was that his tissues would gradually become transparent, and his sensitivity to the flow of electrons would increase as he became more transparent. There was no cure, nothing to slow it down, speed it up, change or enhance any of the symptoms - even the greatest doctors, scientists, and computers in the world had struggled with the problem for over a thousand years.

Wyce continued to reflect on how wonderful his life had been as a result. He had married, had children, and had endured watching his "normal" children leave to see the world. He painfully watched as his lovely wife of 145 years vanished before his eyes. He hoped he would still be able to sense her flow of electrons, but she simply vanished. The other pains in his long life would be when the yearly storms brought lightning strikes. The pain was intense when there was a strike. The storm bunkers would help some but not enough. He also remembered the storms of pleasure. The lights that danced and glowed blue and green in the Northern night skies of wintertime. The ancient books called them Auroras.

He closed his eyes as night brought its darkness, and he reached out to feel the forest around him. His almost invisible hands clutched the damp leaves and the underlying dirt. His only disconcerting thought would be what would happen when he vanished. Where would he go? What would it be like? Would he just cease to exist? Would his mind continue or would his electrons flow into this thick forest carpet around him? He remembered he once read in the ancient Holy Word that the dead are conscious of nothing at all. Would he actually be dead? He didn't know, but he didn't care. He could feel the flow of the forest and a tingle from the dancing auroras above. There was no pain. Only the flow of life through the forest. He gazed at where he gripped the fallen leaves and needles of the trees. The outlined shape of his hands faded, showing only the clump of dirt and leaves. It was time - his time. He gave one last visible smile as his clothing fell to the ground and mingled with the floor of the forest.

—

The Pendant

What I loved about writing this story is that I didn't know where it was going to lead me. All I had at the beginning was the main character and her finding a pendant with a very special ability. There was a lot of research that went into it and I received a great education by the time the story was done. Oh, and I sure wish I had one of these pendants!

***

Kristi was intrigued by the design of the necklace and the dangling pendant. It looked old — like something out of the historical romance novels she liked to read. "What can you tell me about this?" She pointed at it and tapped on the thick glass of the display case.

The proprietor of the pawnshop lifted the necklace from the display case. "Just got this in yesterday, Miss." He gently lifted the pendant and chain off a stand and laid it out slowly onto a black velvet cloth. "An interesting fellow in a tux and top hat came in with it. He didn't talk much. All he said is it was time to pass it on.

The tightly weaved silver chains of the necklace glittered against the black of the velvet. The pendant was a circular silver cast of a feline animal with very tiny jewels for its eyes. Its body circled around a multi-faceted translucent gem with a layer of light blue at the surface turning to a deeper blue inside. The tail of the cat curved around an axle for two optic lenses of glass hovering over the top of the center gem — magnifying the deep sparkle of blue from within. Kristi slid the top lens off to the side and then the bottom lens, revealing the smallness of the center gem. "Wow. The lenses make the center gem look like it's several carats.

"Yeah. It's actually one-third of a carat.

Kristi had to have it. There was no doubt or question about it. "I'll take it!

The proprietor paused for a few seconds, startled by the lack of discussion about price. "Um, okay. That will be thirteen hundred," he stated cautiously, already wondering if the price would scare her off.

"Fine," she replied, pulling her parent's credit card out of her purse and flipping it down onto the glass counter. She knew it was tapping into her allocated college funds, but she didn't care.

Throughout the day at college, Kristi was thrilled to talk about her new found necklace. Everyone commented how unique it was, where she found it, and how much was it worth. By the time she arrived at her dorm room she was worn out from the reiterations of descriptions, but still excited about finding it. She found herself unconsciously toying with it throughout the evening while studying her homework. Her roommate had asked if she could borrow it for her date tonight, but there was no way Kristi was going to let it go.

"Ugh, finals," she exclaimed. She went downstairs to the dorm kitchen and made herself an espresso to help get through a late night of cramming the books. Continuing to play with the pendant, she unconsciously twirled the magnifying lenses to one side while feeling the texture of the gemstone in the middle. Applying a little pressure to feel the bevels of the gem, she felt it give a little, and it sank down into its base with a click.

Kristi was instantly and totally engulfed in darkness. She felt panic start to set in, wondering if she was having a stroke or some other type of health issue. She felt like she was floating with nothing beneath her. Lifting her hand to her forehead, she found some comfort in being able to feel her own hand and forehead. Looking down, she could see a very faint glow of blue from the center of the pendant. Again, another sense of relief at knowing her vision was okay as well. She grasped the pendant with one hand and slowly felt for the center gem. Rubbing a thumb over it, she applied slight pressure until it clicked.

The cup of espresso was still steaming in front of her. She looked around at the kitchen area. A couple students were sitting at a table enjoying a snack and talking. No one noticed anything different. She wasn't sure if she should mention what just happened to her or not. Actually, she wasn't really sure what happened. She grabbed her espresso and nervously headed back to her room.

She sat down at her desk, took the necklace off, and laid it down. Her hands were shaking as she moved the pendant lenses around and gently touched the center gem. The deep blue tint seemed to glow more as she touched it. She pressed the gem. Nothing happened. Maybe she imagined the whole thing. She shook her head. It was too vivid. Had to be real. She put the necklace back on, took a deep breath, and pressed the gem.

The darkness enveloped her again. She quickly pressed the gem and found herself sitting at her desk, facing her laptop computer. The time on the computer clock said 9:47 pm. She pushed the gem and entered back into the darkness. She felt disoriented, like she was floating in outer space, but without any stars. There was nothing to touch except herself, her clothing, and the necklace. She cradled the pendant in the palm of her hand and raised it up to eye level. It glowed a deep blue and pulsed slightly, like a heartbeat. She released it and watched it slowly drop to the center of the necklace chain, below her neck.

Staring out into the darkness she tried feeling around and then attempted to spin around. There was no sense of direction and she couldn't feel anything. There was nothing to stand on or sit on. Her legs dangled loosely. "Hello?" The sound of her voice sent a chill through her. It was flat sounding, like being in a sound proof room, with no echoes, no other sounds. She waited but didn't know why - she just felt she needed to wait.

After what seemed like an hour or more, there was no change in the darkness, even though her eyes were fully adapted to the dark. Only a slight glow from the gem in the pendant could be seen when she occasionally held it up. She pressed the gem. Her desk and computer instantly appeared. She was still sitting in her chair. The time on the computer clock still showed 9:47 pm. "What?" The computer clock eventually incremented to 9:48, proving to her it was still working — time was still progressing. Just not when she was in the… She wasn't sure what to call it. The Darkness, she decided.

Her medical schooling research glared at her from the computer screen. "Dang — test tomorrow. This is going to take me all night." An idea suddenly occurred to her. "Sleep," she stated to herself while grabbing the pendant and gazing at it. She looked back up at the computer clock showing 9:53 and pressed the center gem of the pendant. The glow from the computer screen faded from her eyes as she entered the darkness. Perfect for sleeping, she thought. Even though she wanted to sleep, she found the lack of noise and gravity was uncomfortable. She continued to stare into the darkness. After what seemed like several hours, she started to hear and feel her heart beating. Flashes of images from her mind started to play out in the darkness. She knew the lack of sensory input was enhancing her hearing and her mind was playing the images. Eventually, she managed to fall asleep.

Kristi awoke with a panic. Her sleep had been so deep, she had forgotten where she was. It took her a few seconds to remember. Nothing had changed. She still floated in the dark. The sounds of her own body echoed in her ears. She felt rested, peaceful, and content — almost like a womb or a cocoon. She chuckled at the thought while grasping the pendant and pressing the center gem.

The brightness of the computer screen and the light in the room was startling. It took Kristi a few seconds before she could focus her eyes on the monitor. The clock read 9:48 p.m. "Wow." She laughed. She had managed to get a good night's sleep without loosing any time. Her coffee was still warm. She giggled while pondering the possibilities. She dove into her studies and spent the entire night preparing for her test.

The college medical exam was a breeze. Kristi used the pendant anytime she felt stumped by a question. She would ponder the issue while in the dark and return to fill out the answer. She managed to actually finish the exam a good thirty minutes before the rest of the students. She then wished she had the ability to speed up time instead of having to wait for everyone else.

—

The rest of medical school was a breeze, thanks to the

pendant. Kristi used it at every opportunity. Her friends and teachers commented on how much she had changed. She was so positive, always had so much energy, and was able to get so much done. After getting many questions on why she always wore the pendant, she started keeping it in her purse, or in her pocket. She had tried under a sweater once but discovered it wouldn't work if the gem didn't have direct contact with her fingers when being pressed. She also became very possessive and worried about other people even looking at it. It became a significant concern and she found herself worrying excessively about what she would do if she ever lost it, or if it ever quit working. Her worry became so bad she finally decided to lock it away, and she tried going for weeks without relying on it. She finally found a balance and would only use it when necessary, and not for every single convenience.

The pendant became especially valuable when she started her hospital residency as a surgeon in the Emergency Room. She would breeze through the long shifts and would "blank" out to calm her nerves in a very stressful emergency, or to have more time to think about the situation. She soon gained a reputation as one of the most brilliant surgeons on staff. She felt bad about all the praise and recognition. She was just like anyone else, aside from the ability to take more time to work out her solutions. Time to think was her only advantage. Her attempts at taking a laptop or smartphone with her didn't work out very well. There was no internet or cell coverage in the darkness. Her research was limited to the data she could take with her.

Years after her residency and becoming the Senior Director of Surgery, the most critical emergency in her life happened. A twelve-year-old girl had come into the ER suffering from an epileptic seizure during her shift. Medication and intubation had stopped the seizures, and an MRI showed a strange parasite wrapped around the girl's cerebral cortex just below the base of the brain. No one had ever seen anything like it and the staff looked to Kristi for an answer. She panicked and pressed the gem.

The darkness was soothing and calming. Floating in the darkness, she pondered how she could save the girl's life. Staring off into the darkness, the images of the MRI floated out in front of her, firmly burned into her mind. A blue glow appeared in the middle of the visions. It drew closer and became brighter. She couldn't determine if she was imagining it or if the blue light was really there.

The light grew into a box shape, which became a rectangle, and increased to the size of a door opening. Kristi could feel gravity slowly come into normal force and she was able to stand up in front of the blue rectangle. She reached out toward the box, but before she could make contact with it, the glowing blue light dissolved to show a large white room with people waiting and staring at her. Each person had a slight outline of a bluish tint surrounding their skin. They all became excited at her appearance before them.

One blue tinted man stepped forward, extended his hand toward her. "It's okay, Kristi. You can come through. We'll explain everything.

Strangely, she felt comfortable with taking the man's hand as she stepped through the opening and into the room. It looked like a medical laboratory, much like those at the hospital. Though everything had the same slight bluish tint — everything, even the floor.

"My name is Fibri. I have been your monitor." The man guided her to a large flat screen display on a wall. It showed images of everything Kristi had seen of the young girl back at the hospital.

"My monitor?" She paused while staring at the display. "I'm not sure I understand."

"I'm sorry if this is all sudden and a bit overwhelming." He pointed at the display. "We are all here to help you with the girl, and with your species." He pointed at the display and made a gesture with his hand. The display changed to an image of Kristi floating in nothing while sleeping. "During your visits, I have been able to monitor your mentality."

"My mentality?" Kristi felt a slight pang of panic. Is this real? Am I dreaming this?

Fibri touched her hand gently and she felt a warmth and calmness wash over her. He continued. "I assure you, you are not dreaming. We are not of your universe, but we are here to help. A hired traveler placed this device…" He pointed to the pendant. "in your environment. You were attracted to it for a very specific reason. When you visit us," He pointed at the image of her floating. "we download your images, emotions, and experiences. This is the only way we can interact with your species. Everything you see here," He swept one hand around and Kristi looked at the people and the room, all with the slight bluish glow. "is a projection for your benefit."

"Wow." She had a tough time comprehending all that Fibri was telling her. Yet, she knew, and felt, in her inner being, it was all true. She faced the display, which had changed back to the view of the young girl and the MRI scans. You want to help me with the girl?"
"That is correct," Fibri replied and turned back toward the display. He gestured with one hand and

the display changed to show a rotating image of the parasite which had attached itself to the young girl's cerebral cortex. "This is an Agmar. It's a very dangerous and invasive species which has recently dropped into the atmosphere of your planet. If allowed to proliferate, it will eventually consume every living being on your planet. The Agmar feeds on fluids in the body, starting with the spinal fluids. As the body starts to die, the Agmar releases hundreds of its offspring, at a viral level. Others will become infected, and it will spread. The girl will die in around two of your rotations. We project total annihilation of your species within six months. There will be others infected due to your planet passing through a drifting stream of Agmar."

Kristi was stunned, sick to her stomach, and almost vomited. Fibri touched her on the arm and provided a comforting sense of concern. She felt composure and confidence wash over her. Realizing the sense came from the touch, she smiled at Fibri while replying. "Thank you." Looking back at the display, she asked. "How do I stop it?"

"We will give you instructions on how you can remove the Agmar with your existing technologies. You'll not only save the girl, but you'll be saving your entire race from this pestilence. However, there is a request from us for the use of this knowledge."

"A request?" She paused. "As in a price to pay?"

"We have no need of financial units. It is irrelevant to our species. What we need is help from those who have this knowledge and experience. We need you to come back to us and assist us."

"Ah. You mean instead of sleeping, I could come and help you?"

"Unfortunately no. The next time you use the pendant, you will be here permanently. You cannot go back."

Kristi paused for a long minute while observing the faces of the various people, or aliens, in the room. The looks were of anxiety, anticipation, concern, and possibly a little desperation. "Um, I…" She paused. "Can I have time to think about it?"

"Of course." He replied while giving a look and nod to the others. "You can still take our knowledge of this resolution with you. Just be sure to save the girl, and share the solution before you come back."

"I understand," Kristi responded solemnly.

Fibri and his team showed Kristi the necessary processes for detaching and killing the Agmar. While it was fairly detailed, it did utilize technology which could easily be found at the hospital. They reviewed the process multiple times until Kristi was certain she had the process memorized. Certain that Kristi was now capable of saving the young girl, each member of Fibri's team approached her, held her hand, and stated, 'Alams kre damas mouel.' Fibri was the last in line to hold her hand and repeated the statement.

"Is that a 'So long and good luck?' Kristi asked.

"It means: May our knowledge help you to be true to your efforts." Fibri
waved a hand and a portal opened up into the darkness behind Kristi.

Tears came to her eyes as she turned and faced the opening. Turning back toward Fibri, she gave him a kiss on the cheek. "Thank you for giving me this knowledge and ability to save our race."

"If you come back to us you can also help to save others in our universe," Fibri stated and gestured toward the portal.

Kristi stepped through the opening and was instantly swallowed by the darkness. She allowed herself to float awhile, to ponder all she had learned, and to consider her options. When she felt she was ready to step back into the emergency room with the little girl she pressed the center of the pendant.

Sounds of the emergency room abruptly flooded her. The nurses, assistants, and other doctors were staring, waiting for her decisions. She had it all down in her mind. "I need this girl moved back to the MRI. Prep her for a scan. No injections except for the saline. Myers, go to the pharmacy and get me an ounce of colloidal silver. If they don't have it, drive to the drug store and get it. Sue, I'll need a laser guide bracket. Jones, get video. We're going to record this." She paused and noticed the team was stunned by the sudden list of instructions. "Stat! That's now, people!"

The various team members scattered to their assignments while Kristi leaned over the young sedated girl and lightly brushed her hair off her face. "Hang in there sweetie. We're going to make you better."

Kristi watched the monitors while the young girl was being scanned by the MRI. A gray-haired doctor stepped up beside her. "So, what is it, Kristi?" He asked while checking the images on the monitors.

"Ah, Director Ferguson. It's an invasive species." She replied calmly.

"Excuse me? An invasive species? How do you know?"

"In all your training, your years of experience — have you ever seen anything like this?" She pointed at the MRI image on the monitors.

He stepped closer to the monitors and studied the images for a few minutes before responding. "No, I guess I haven't." He paused for another minute. "What's your plan?"

"Well, this specific creature is highly sensitive to light. Normal exposure will cause it become ill and will slow its aggression. But to kill it, we'll increase its sensitivity, then we bombard it with laser light. This will overwhelm its defenses and it will die. Any other process will cause it to release toxins and kill the patient."

"I see." The doc contemplated Kristi's diagnosis for a few minutes. "How do you increase it's sensitivity to light?"

"Colloidal Silver injection into the patient's bloodstream. We give it a couple hours to fully saturate and via an incision, we expose the parasite to a carbon dioxide gas laser. As it dies, it will release its grip on her cerebral cortex, and we extract it via the same incision."

"How do you know this will work?" The doctor removed his glasses and gazed intently at Kristi.

"I stumbled across some research leading me to this conclusion." She could tell he was skeptical. "It's very conclusive."

"Why have I not come across this research?"

"Do Hospital Vice Presidents have time to read all the new research?"

"I suppose not." He put his glasses back on and turned his attention back to the monitors. "I hope you're right. I expect to see your papers on this procedure, ready for release, in my email by tomorrow morning."

"What?" She gasped. "Those usually take a week or two for me to submit. Why the big rush?"

"CDC has reported twenty-one new infestations matching this one and no one has any clue of what to do about it." He gazed back at her over the top of his glasses. "I guess they don't read the same research you do."

The young girl was strapped and anchored face down. Various tubes and sensors were bundled together next to the girl's neck, feeding vital oxygen, anesthesia, and monitoring the girl's vitals. Kristi and her team were fully gowned, and the cameras were recording. She began her dialog for the video. "Our patient is a twelve-year-old female. She has a parasitic infestation attached to her cerebral cortex, just below the brain. The parasite, which I'm calling an Agmar, is approximately eight inches long, elongated, similar to a leech in shape. MRI scan shows a texture of scales, similar to a fish. The patient was injected with thirty ccs of drug store quality colloidal silver, four hours prior to surgery. The colloidal increases sensitivity to light and the Agmar absorbs it from the patient. We will now incise the patient at the base of the skull."

Aside from a small rectangle area of skin, the young girl was draped in a light blue surgical paper. Several bright spotlights were focused on the spot. "Stand by swab and spreader," Kristi instructed her team as she slowly cut through the young girl's skin and epidural layers. An aide swabbed at the oozing blood and fluids while Kristi exchanged her scalpel for a titanium spreader. She carefully inserted it and slowly released it against the sides of the incision. She continued for the cameras. "Incision is three inches and spreader has been inserted. I'm now tilting the spreader to provide a visual of the Agmar." She gently pulled on the handle of the spreader, causing the skin to lift on one side and expose a view into the base of the skull where the cortex anchored to the brain. Pulling a small, digital camera closer to the opening, she checked one of the monitors to make sure the camera view had the image on the screen. Various gasps were uttered by the team as the shape of the Agmar came into view.

"This is the tail and main body of the Agmar. The body is wrapped around half of the cortex and the head is anchored to the cortex just under the base of the brain." One of the aides pulled a sliding anchor bracket over the incision and attached a clamp onto the end of the spreader. Kristi released her grip of the spreader. Another aide attached a laser mounted in an aluminum frame to the anchor bracket. "We're mounting a carbon dioxide gas laser to a suspended anchor bracket. We'll be using a red laser guide to pinpoint the gas laser before firing."

The team watched the monitors as red crosshairs showed up on the body of the Agmar. "Preparing to power up the gas laser. The source energy will be at 300 milliwatts. The beam will be defocused to create a wider beam on the surface of the Agmar." Kristi flipped down a laser protection shield over her clear face shield. "Beginning laser ignite in three, two, one."

Aside from the sound of the heart monitor and the assisted breathing system, there were no other sounds. It seemed the entire team was holding their breath as they watched the intense white beam hit the Agmar and expand from a pinpoint to the size of a dime on the creature's scales. Everyone gasped as they saw the Agmar shrivel and slowly uncurl from around the cerebral cortex.

"Disengage the laser," Kristi stated. "I'm reaching into the incision with a suction tube set on the minimal amount of force." She slowly moved the tube into the incision and attached it to the tail of the Agmar. There was no further movement from the creature as she slowly tugged and maneuvered it through the incision. "I'm slowly pulling the Agmar out through the incision. Prepare for a saline wash."

One of the aides held a pint size bottle of saline fluid with a directional spout close to the incision. Another aide slid the anchor bracket with the laser away from the patient. Kristi pulled the Agmar clear of the incision and dropped it into a stainless steel pan. A clear lid was clamped down over the pan. There was no movement from the Agmar and it shrunk a little after hitting the pan. "The Agmar is contained. Flush the incision, examine for debris, then flush again before closing."

The team applauded and praised Kristi and each other. "That's a wrap. Get the video over to the distribution office and out to the other hospitals immediately." A voice stated from an intercom, sounding like Dr. Ferguson.

Kristi checked on the young girl several hours later. She was conscious and communicating with various nurses and doctors. Her parents heaped praise and admiration on Kristi, though she humbly felt it was undeserved. She only did what she was taught by Fibri. As she stepped out of the girl's room and walked through the hallway, she continued to receive praise from staff and strangers. She paused at a TV in a waiting room as a news program talked about the mystery parasite infecting people around the world and the surgeon who came up with the innovative process for killing and removing the Agmar's.

"Better get used to it." Dr. Ferguson stated while walking up and standing beside her. "You're a celebrity."

She cringed at his statement. She didn't do this for fame or popularity. She was here to help heal people.

"We scheduled a press conference for this afternoon."

He paused and glanced at her for a reaction, then continued. "CDC is reporting over a thousand cases around the world. The press is asking for you to be available for questions."

Kristi felt the panic building up inside. "It's all in the video. Just give it to them. They can learn from that." She shakily replied while staring at the TV.

"We did, but they want to meet the 'Agmar Doctor'. Just imagine the book deal you can get from this."

"What time is the press conference?" She gently caressed the edges of the pendant.

"Five thirty. Just in time for the evening news. Oh, CNN said they would be here as well." He turned away from the TV in time to see Kristi heading out of the waiting room.

— —

Dr. Ferguson stood behind a lectern positioned in front of the hospital logo, next to the front entrance. A group of microphones had been strapped and zip tied to the top — each with their own station logo showing, and the most prominent was CNN. He paused for a long minute, waiting for the onslaught of camera flashes to die down. It also gave him more time to formulate how he would break the news to the media.

"Good afternoon." He stated while shuffling a few index cards. "I'm Dr. Ferguson, Vice President of Medical Operations for Southwest University Hospital." He paused again and glanced off to the side, hoping to see that Kristi had changed her mind and was willing to speak. She wasn't there. "I know that you're all here to meet our Senior Director of Surgery, Doctor Kristina Mendosa. Thanks to a discovery by Dr. Mendosa, we have been able to find a way to remove infestations of a new parasitic worm called an Agmar. As you know, this infestation has affected thousands of people around the world and was totally unheard of until a week ago. The process for the removal of the Agmar has been documented and videos have been streamed to all major medical facilities around the world." The VP pointed to a video monitor off to the left side of the lectern. He made another glance to the side, confirming what he already expected — Kristi was still not there.

—

Mir'zea floated in the darkness, pondering how he would tackle the infestation which attacked his clan. The tribe looked to him for healing and solutions to all of their sicknesses. This was something he had never seen before. He panicked in their moment of greatest need and used the pendant dangling from his neck to escape to the darkness. He needed to think, to work out a solution, as he had done so many times before. He was thankful for the barter he had made for the pendant, so many rotations ago. As he reflected on the sickness in his tribe, a thin blue rectangle suddenly appeared in the darkness in front of him.

Mir'zea could feel gravity slowly come into normal force and he was able to stand up in front of the blue rectangle. He reached out toward it, wondering if he could touch it. The glowing blue light dissolved to show a large compartment with various intellects waiting and staring at him. Each intellect had a very slight outline of a bluish tint surrounding their skin. He knew they were able to see him as well.

One intellect stepped forward, extending a hand toward him. "It's okay, Mir'zea. You can come through. We'll explain everything."

Strangely, he felt comfortable with taking a hold of the intellect's protrusion and stepping through the opening into the compartment. It looked like a healing tent, much like what he had been used to during his training. Though everything had the same slight bluish tint — everything, even the floor.

"My name is Kristi. I have been your monitor." The intellect guided him to a large display on one side of the compartment. It showed images of everything Mir'zea had seen of the infected warrior back at his ward.

"My monitor?" He paused while staring at the display. "I'm not sure I understand."

"I'm sorry if this is all sudden and a bit overwhelming." She pointed at the display. "We are all here to help you with the warrior, and with your species." She pointed at the display and made a gesture with her hand. The display changed to an image of Mir'zea floating in nothing while sleeping. "During your visits, I have been able to monitor your mentality."

"My mentality?" Mir'zea was confused.

Kristi touched his hand gently and he felt a warmth and calmness wash over him. She continued. "We are not of your universe, but we are here to help. A hired traveler bartered with you and gave you this device." She pointed at the pendant on his chest and smiled.

—

UNDISCOVERED

Zap 'Em

Every now and then I'll write a short poem or something for a friend in a thank you card. However, as a story goes, this is the shortest story I have ever written. Enjoy.

***

Josh wasn't sure if the money he paid for the ZapEm

app on his smartphone was really worth it until he got on the 9:32 a.m. bus to downtown Seattle. Sitting across from him was an unruly kid of around nineteen, with music blaring from his earbuds, torn clothes, and a stench that would peel the paint off walls. People around him moved away as much as they could. Josh opened the ZapEm app, pointed the smartphone camera, and tapped the red button. The applause and shouts were amazing as the unruly kid disappeared.

—

Air Born - Do You Dream of Flying?

After thousands of years, the ancient 18th of Ahmose are still on the hunt for the secret of flight, forcing Avitorians to hide in fear. Facing the threat of capture, Leif's dreams are shattered when he is forced to decide between hiding or embracing his heritage.

This Sci-fi/Fantasy YA novel is available in print at all major book stores and from Amazon.com

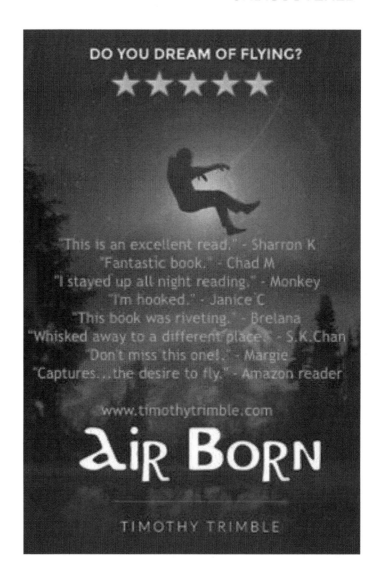

***

The following is an excerpt from my first full-length novel. The story started from a short story I wrote as a contest entry for a local writers convention. The title of the story was, "Love Is In the Air." Okay, it was a cheesy title, I admit. However, when my editor read it, she told me I had to stop everything I was doing and turn it into a novel. Well, I didn't stop my work on Zegin's Abduction, but I did start mapping out the entire story line for Air Born.

After three years of work, from concept to print, I'm very pleased with how this story is being received. The average rating on Amazon is five stars and the reviews sometimes bring me to tears. I'm so very grateful to the fans for the love, pictures, and support they are showing this story. Here's a short peek of the first scene in the first chapter.

***

CHAPTER ONE - ALL I WANNA DO

"We do not write our history for fear it would be discovered. Though we cherish our heritage and the gift we have been blessed with, we are to remain vague when it comes to documenting. There are those who seek to obtain what we have, regardless of the cost. Extinction is what we fear - the loss of our beauty, and our sense for peace." (The Guide to Preservation. Author unknown.)

--

(Year: 1995)

Angela loved the way her hair flowed in the wind as she flew through the pristine and cool night air. "All I wanna do is have some fun…" blared on her earbuds attached to the portable cassette player secured around her upper arm. She slowly drifted through the desert canyon air without glancing at the mountain peaks to her right and left. Her knowledge of each turn, nook, and cranny was permanently burned into her seventeen year old subconscious memory. She bobbed her head and silently mouthed the lyrics along with Sheryl. This was, after all, her own personal playground.

"So what if it happened to be in the middle of Joshua Tree National Park?" she had defiantly stated to her older sister, before heading out for the night of flying. "It's a secluded canyon. The only people who show up are old L.A. hippies looking for a place to get stoned. If they did manage to see me, they'll think they're just trippin. It's no big deal." She said in defense with one foot out the door.

She shut out the discussion with her sister and gazed at the sky. She enjoyed the stars the most. Moonless nights were always the best - easier to see the millions of pinpoints in the Milky Way, and less of a chance of being seen. She slowly came to a stop and hovered on her back while gazing at the stars, wondering if her ancestors came from the heavens or were just another type of the human species. She had asked her uncle Georgeo during one of his rare visits a few months before. He didn't know, but he told her that he liked to think they came from the stars. Two Avitorians - male and female - seeking someplace to colonize. Too bad the humans were already here, he would chuckle. He told her they stayed because they saw something intriguing in the humans. Compassion, love, and a thirst for knowledge. The few who spoke of peace and hope out shone those who strive for power and riches. This was what kept the Avitorians on earth. Once they made their decision, the ability to return to their home world or to seek out another place to colonize had been taken away. How or why - he didn't know. Of course, Georgeo reminded her it was just a story and he was not sure if it was really true or not.

Draco the dragon was directly overhead tonight. She traced the shape of the constellation with her finger down past Ursa Minor toward the body of Ursa Major. She drifted her hand from side to side in rhythm with Sheryl Crow's guitar. She rolled over and glanced at the blackness of the ground; she estimated it was a little over 400 feet to the valley floor below. By dead reckoning she triangulated the 3600 foot peak to her right and the 3700 foot peak on her left. With the subtle light from a million stars she could make out the the course of the dry creak bed running West to East and another one intersecting from the South straight below. It was a popular intersection for weekend campers, but tonight there was no sign of life below. No campfires, no lanterns, no glow of cigarettes (or joints) as campers would find comfort in a drag of unhealthful smoke. She wondered why anyone would smoke. She remembered the lesson from the blackened tissue on display in last year's biology class. Tonight was Wednesday. *Bah*. I wish I didn't have school tomorrow, she thought.

Drifting West, Angela moved past the creek junction below and the peaks now behind, toward an opening in the canyon. The dry lake bed was completely surrounded by mountains. Three miles long and a mile wide - it was the perfect place for her to hover and soak in the immensity of the night sky. She stopped in her favorite spot and rolled over to face the sky. She really wanted to stay long enough to see the constellation Orion stick it's head over the Eastern horizon, but that would mean staying up most of the

night, and risking the brightness of the revealing
moon rise. She would never hear the end of it from
her sister if she did. *Just a few more minutes and I'll
head back.* She watched the star Deneb so intently
she could sense it's movement as it inched across the
sky. The clack of Angela's cassette tape player
startled her as it clicked off after the last song. She
always felt uneasy with even the slightest noise in the
middle of such a pristinely quiet night in the desert.

Suddenly, she felt unusually warm. *Now that's weird.*
She glanced at the surrounding land marks and
noticed that she was starting to descend. Rolling over
to face the dry lake bed, she noticed there were new
shadows cast by the starlight in a spot where
normally there was nothing but sand. She banked
steeply to her right and headed toward the Northern
cliffs. The warmth was gone and she regained
altitude. Her curiosity prompted her to hover feet first
and turn, facing the middle of the lake bed. Multiple
shadows moved and once again she felt her body get
warm. The air around her was still cool, but her body
itself was feeling warm - almost like a fever. She felt
control of her altitude slip as she again began
descending. At the same moment she was blinded by
light from below. Bathed in bright white she
instinctively covered her eyes with her hands hoping
she could get a glimpse between her fingers. She
continued descending. She knew if she was forced to

go to ground she would not be able to run as fast as she could fly. She could feel panic rising in her chest.

The adrenaline gave her strength to resist the descent. She turned away from the lights and headed for the canyon as fast as she could. *They saw me! Who are they? Why are they here?* Questions flooded her mind as she tried to stifle the panic. Forcing herself to focus, she dove toward the canyon entrance in an attempt to gain some needed speed and momentum. *I've got to get out of here and get safe. Where was the heat coming from and why did I stop flying?* Her mind was racing. She could hear distant shouts and the sound of some kind of vehicle engine firing up behind her. It sounded like a VW - possibly a dune buggy. She didn't want to chance looking back to find out. The lights was still shinning on her, but they were dimmer as she reached the canyon opening. She skimmed the ground barely avoiding the snag of the sage and shadowed brush along the valley floor. With the increased speed and momentum, she shot straight into the night sky and out of the beams of the lights.

"You fools! You frigging idiots! Get the light back on her, now!" The woman screamed at the two men as they jumped to the task and slid into the bucket seats of the four seater sand rail. The woman was crouched in the back gripping the back of a strange looking cannon, in cables and coiled copper wrappings around the barrel. The ribbed balloon tires dug into the sand as the driver gunned the gas. A row of flood lights came on across the top of the roll bar above the driver's head. The man in the passenger seat struggled with the portable spot light as they raced after the escaping flier.

The woman was knocked back into the seat by the acceleration. She quickly stood up and grabbed the twin grips of the cannon, hanging on with all her might as the vehicle bounced along the dry lake bed. She managed her balance and pressed the button on the microphone clipped to her shoulder. "Coming your way." Two clicks over the speaker acknowledged the listener on the other radio received her message.

Angela leveled off at 3600 feet even with the highest peak off to the North of the canyon wall. She glanced back over her shoulder at the approaching buggy with it's bouncing flood lights and a single spot light beam searching the sky. Her luck was holding, they hadn't locked her in, at least not yet. Her heart was pounding; she thought it would burst. She turned and along the edge of the canyon as it gently snaked through an S shaped curve. *I've got to calm down and get my senses.* She knew the canyon would straighten out before reaching the creek junction, at least that would give her a vantage point to see the buggy approach. *I could go straight up and just get some distance, but it would be easier to see me. I usually fly East. This time I'll go South. The old creek climbs into the mountains and I can disappear there. No way they can follow me.* She descended toward the creek bed at an angle, building up her momentum.

The sand rail reached the canyon entrance, bouncing and sliding left as the driver dodged the rocks and Joshua Trees. The man with the spot light scanned the sky as he tried to compensate for the sudden movements of the sand rail.

"Crank it up to fifteen hundred, Matt!" The woman stated into the microphone. "Twelve hundred isn't enough." She let go of the mic and grabbed the back of the cannon with both hands. "Try to get us through that S turn without flipping us over," she causticly barked at the driver.

Angela could hear the roar of the buggy entering the turn of the canyon. The sounds of the engine echoed and reverberated off the canyon walls; making it sound like an army of vehicles. She turned and caught a quick glance of the lights flickering on the mountain sides, casting dancing shadows of

sagebrush along the sides of the creek bed. Jack
rabbits scattered in terror at the sound of approaching
vehicles and a once pursuing bobcat turned tail and
retreated to the shadows. She double backed toward
the straight section of the dry creek bed, skimming a
few feet above the sand as fast as she could. She saw
the junction of the Southern creek coming up quickly
as the light from the approaching buggy caught her
while she was preparing to fly toward escape. As she
started banking into the turn she glimpsed another
vehicle parked just East of her path. Lights beamed
from the vehicle blinding her before she could cover
her eyes. Realizing she had been cornered she reacted
instinctively and shot straight up into the air, flying as
fast as her heart and adrenaline would permit.

Immediately she felt the heat again. She darted
sideways, gaining altitude trying her best get out of
the heat, but it was still there - following her as she
flew. The earbuds from her portable Walkman began
to bake in her ears. She ripped them out as she jerked
the player off her arm, letting them fall away to the
ground below. She turned to look at the approaching
buggy coming down the straight section of the creek
bed. The spotlight from the buggy swung across the
sky to meet her. She turned around and saw the
converging buggy with lights blaring. She was
slowing down and couldn't gather enough strength to
continue flying. The heat doubled in intensity and she

could feel pain burning in her bones, radiating out into her muscles. She spun around, hoping somehow the maneuver might relieve the pain from the heat, but without any success. She was loosing altitude, falling toward the intersection of the creek bed. The pain was becoming unbearable. She was starting to free fall, plummeting the remaining distance to the ground.

Why are they doing this to me? I'm going to die. Confusion and fear filled her thoughts as she continued to fall like a wounded bird to the ground. Just as she braced for impact, the heat disappeared. She hung there, spinning slowly in the air, somehow she had managed to stop her descent. She was just feet from the ground and she was just hovering. She felt the spinning slow and stop as both vehicles converged upon her - their lights blaring, making it hard to see the occupants. The seconds she hovered seemed like hours. Her senses were on full overload, her heart pumping rapidly, and she realized she was hyperventilating; she felt on the verge of passing out.

"Leave me alone! Go away!" She screamed as loud as she could. *What are they waiting for?* She wondered. She looked up and saw the star Deneb flickering in the darkness, as if winking at her to tell her everything would be okay. She could hear a woman speaking as the men got out of their vehicles.

She started to ascend again, but was instantly hit by the intense heat. Her bones felt like pins of red hot steel, melting from the heat.

"Please. Stop!" she cried out. Curling up in a ball she closed her eyes and fell to the ground. The sand softened the blow. Although the heat had disappeared, she was too weak and exhausted to fly away. She slowly stretched out face down in the sand. The coolness of the sand was oddly comforting. She heard footsteps approaching as she tried to roll over when suddenly, she felt a sharp prick to her neck. All she could think of was *scorpions* as her mind grew fuzzy and she fell into a fitful sleep.

—

UNDISCOVERED

Book Selfies

If you enjoy any of these stories, feel free to join in with the rest of my fans and readers who have sent me their book selfies.

You can send your pictures via Instagram to TimothyTrimble via

www.instagram.com/TimothyTrimble or just tag @TimothyTrimble when you post.

UNDISCOVERED

Other Books By Timothy

UNDISCOVERED - A collection of short stories
ISBN-13: 978-1797747507

Air Born - Do You Dream of Flying? ISBN-10:
1536873292
ISBN-13: 978-1536873290

Zegin's Adventures in Epsilon ISBN/EAN13:
1-50326-243-X/9781503262430

Adventures in Flight Simulator, Microsoft Press
ISBN: 1-55615-582-4

FileMaker Pro Design & Scripting for Dummies,
Wiley Publications - ISBN: 0-471-78648-9

Coming Soon!

Air Born in Spanish!

Air Storm - Do You Dream of Falling?

55169933R00076

Made in the USA
Columbia, SC
12 April 2019